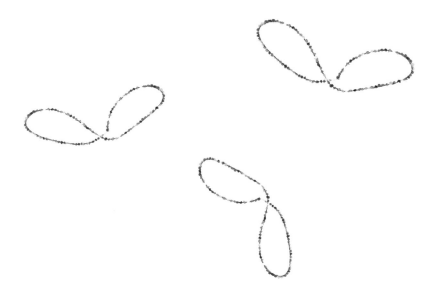

the magic beads

Written by Susin Nielsen-Fernlund

with illustrations by Geneviève Côté

To Göran: Oändligt är vårt äventyr.   S.F.

For Suzanne Nepveu, a.k.a. Madame Idélire,
who shares her own magic beads with such
inspired generosity.   G.C.

First published in 2007 by Simply Read Books Inc.
www.simplyreadbooks.com

Text copyright © 2007 Susin Nielsen-Fernlund

Illustrations copyright © 2007 Geneviève Côté

We gratefully acknowledge the support of the
Canada Council for the Arts and the BC Arts Council
for our publishing program.

Library and Archives Canada Cataloguing in Publication

Nielsen-Fernlund, Susin, 1964-

   The magic beads / Susin Fernlund-Nielsen ; Genevieve
Cote, illustrator.

ISBN 978-1-894965-47-7

   I. Côté, Geneviève, 1964- II. Title.

PS8577.I37M35 2007   jC813'.54   C2007-900726-0

Design by Steedman Design

10 9 8 7 6 5 4 3 2 1

Printed in Singapore

A portion of the author's royalties will go to the Vi
Fineday family shelter in Vancouver, BC.

the magic beads

Written by Susin Nielsen-Fernlund
with illustrations by Geneviève Côté

Simply Read Books

Lillian had butterflies in her stomach.

It was her first day of second grade in a brand new school in a brand new city.

"Welcome Lillian," said the teacher, Ms. Garcia. "I think you'll enjoy our classroom." She told Lillian about all the things they were working on, then she said, "And every day we have Show and Tell. Your Show and Tell day will be Friday."

The butterflies in her tummy turned into GRASSHOPPERS.

On Tuesday, Jennifer brought in a doll that could talk, crawl and even pee. Kwame brought in a brand-new scooter, and Ms. Garcia let him ride it across the room once to show them how it worked.

The grasshoppers in Lillian's tummy
turned into BUNNY RABBITS.

After school, Lillian walked home. Except
it wasn't really home. It was a family shelter.
Lillian and her mom had a big room in a big
house where some other families were staying,
too. The ladies who worked there were nice.
But you weren't allowed to take food out of
the fridge between meals. And the boy staying
down the hall never put down the toilet seat.

On Wednesday, Freddy brought in a model of a spaceship, built entirely from Lego. Yuko brought in a robotic pet. It barked when she clapped. The children all wanted a turn.

The bunny rabbits in Lillian's tummy
turned into DONKEYS.

That night the ladies who worked in the shelter made lasagna for supper. It was good, but not as good as the lasagna her dad used to make.

Lillian missed him sometimes. They'd moved into the shelter because he had a bad temper, and sometimes he hit her mom and hurt her. They'd left all their things behind. Including Lillian's toys.

"Bring a toy from the shelter," her mother said as she changed out of her nurse's uniform that night.

"The toys here are for babies," Lillian protested. "I don't want them to think I'm a baby. Please mom, couldn't we buy one?"

Lillian's mom stroked her hair. "No Lily, we can't. I'm saving every penny so we can afford the rent our own place. You know that."

That night, Lillian couldn't watch her
favourite show because the boy down
the hall was already watching a show
about cars.

On Thursday, Boris brought in his collection of action figures.
Alison brought in a whoopee cushion. Ms. Garcia pretended not
to see it when she sat down.

The donkeys in Lillian's tummy
turned into BUFFALOS.

"I saw an apartment today," her mother told her that evening. "We should be able to move in at the end of the month."

Lillian stuck her tongue out at her mom when she wasn't looking.

Sometimes she felt mad at her mom for bringing
them here. At home they'd had their own TV and
lots of clothes and toys. And when her dad was in
a good mood, he would call her "My Lily Girl"
and tickle her feet.

Lillian didn't like to remember when he was in a bad mood. But sometimes she couldn't stop herself, and when that happened, she knew why her mom had taken her away.

On Friday the buffalos in Lillian's tummy ran around in circles.

"It's time for Show and Tell," said Ms. Garcia. "Lillian, why don't you start?"

Lillian walked to the centre of the circle and stared at the floor.

"Lillian?" Ms. Garcia said gently.

"I don't have a toy," she said quietly. "But I do have magic beads."

Lillian lifted the string of plastic beads from around her neck. Freddy giggled. Lillian cleared her throat.

"Sometimes they turn into a leash,
so I can walk my pet elephant."

"If there's a monster in my closet,
I can turn my beads into a snake,
which eats the monster."

"If I meet an evil wizard, I can turn them
into a magic wand and cast a spell."

"Or they turn into my tightrope
when I play circus."

Lillian was finished.

The class was silent.

Then suddenly, lots of hands shot up into the air.

"Where did you get them?" asked Kwame.

"Could I get some too?" asked Yuko.

"You could make a circle with them and stand in the middle of it," said Freddy, "and pretend it's a time machine beaming you into the future."

"Or back to the Ancient Egyptians," Jennifer added.

After the bell rang, Alison approached. "I have a purple ribbon at home," she said. "Do you think it could be magic, too?"

"Oh, yes," said Lillian.

"If I bring it tomorrow, would you like to play?"

"Okay," Lillian smiled.

And as she walked home from school that day, Lillian realized that the butterflies, the grasshoppers, the bunny rabbits, the donkeys and the buffalos ...

Were.   All.   Gone.

the end